SEAMUS'S SHORT STORY

For my "big" kids, Scotty and Jack.
And for my "little" friends, Sophia, Thomas,
Olivia and Matteo — HHS

For Leo and Jelena, for laughs, joy and inspiration… — MP

Text copyright © 2017 by Heather Hartt-Sussman
Illustrations copyright © 2017 by Milan Pavlović
Published in Canada and the USA in 2017 by Groundwood Books

Groundwood Books / House of Anansi Press
groundwoodbooks.com

We acknowledge for their financial support of our publishing program
the Canada Council for the Arts, the Ontario Arts Council
and the Government of Canada.

Canada Council Conseil des Arts
for the Arts du Canada

ONTARIO ARTS COUNCIL
CONSEIL DES ARTS DE L'ONTARIO
an Ontario government agency
un organisme du gouvernement de l'Ontario

With the participation of the Government of Canada
Avec la participation du gouvernement du Canada | Canadä

Library and Archives Canada Cataloguing in Publication
Hartt-Sussman, Heather, author
Seamus's short story / Heather Hartt-Sussman; illustrated by Milan Pavlović.
Issued in print and electronic formats.
ISBN 978-1-55498-793-1 (hardcover). — ISBN 978-1-55498-792-4 (pdf)
I. Pavlović, Milan, illustrator II. Title.
PS8615.A757S43 2017   jC813'.6   C2016-908005-6
C2016-908006-4

The illustrations were done in color pencil and ink.
Design by Michael Solomon
Printed and bound in Malaysia

MIX
Paper from
responsible sources
FSC® C012700

SEAMUS'S SHORT STORY

HEATHER HARTT-SUSSMAN

PICTURES BY MILAN PAVLOVIĆ

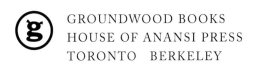

GROUNDWOOD BOOKS
HOUSE OF ANANSI PRESS
TORONTO   BERKELEY

There's no doubt about it.
   Seamus is short.

   And, from where Seamus is standing, the world
appears to be made for tall people.

Tall people can reach things like
elevator buttons to the top floor,

the chocolate milk in the fridge,

the shelf where Dad keeps the TV remote

and horrid pictures of themselves as babies.

Seamus is desperate to find some way
to get the things he can't reach.

He tries a chair (but it's rickety),

a stepladder (but it's wobbly),

and running jumps
(which are hit and miss).

his brother's shoulders
(but they are not quite
high enough)

He'd give his prized
taxidermy collection to
be tall.

He'd give his pirate costume.
He'd even give his two front teeth
(to be fair, they are loose anyway).

One day, while playing dress-up in his mother's closet, Seamus finds a great way to reach new heights…

He tries on his mother's high high-heeled shoes.
He stuffs them with socks.
He tapes them to his ankles.
He even decorates them with his favorite stickers.

Seamus practices wearing the high-heeled shoes in the morning, after school

and even when he is supposed to be in bed!

Eventually, he is steady enough on his feet to go
out into the world.
    When he wears his new shoes, he is able to reach
the top button in the elevator,
the chocolate milk in the fridge,
the TV remote

and finally, finally, he is able to take
down that horrid picture of himself
as a baby.

He teeters from his bedroom to the kitchen.
He totters from the kitchen to the yard.
He traipses from the yard to the neighbor's house
and back again.

Seamus is having a blast.
He feels free. It is wonderful being tall
(except that sometimes his feet hurt).

Then one day he notices some things he wants waaaaaay down below:
a shiny quarter,
the bouncy ball he thought he'd lost,
a pack of gum in Mom's purse,
a beautiful dandelion he would dearly love to pick for her.

So now he must decide.
Up or down?
High or low?

Tall or small?

Seamus deliberates for a long, long time
until he comes up with the answer…

There are times to be tall,

and there are times to be small.

And that's the long and short of it.